HUNTED

OUTRUN. OUTLAST. OUTWIT.

Perilous Pursuits

Edited By Kelly Reeves

First published in Great Britain in 2020 by:

 Young**Writers**®
Est. 1991

Young Writers
Remus House
Coltsfoot Drive
Peterborough
PE2 9BF
Telephone: 01733 890066
Website: www.youngwriters.co.uk

All Rights Reserved
Book Design by Ashley Janson
© Copyright Contributors 2020
Softback ISBN 978-1-83928-559-2

Printed and bound in the UK by BookPrintingUK
Website: www.bookprintinguk.com
YB0437N

FOREWORD

IF YOU'VE BEEN SEARCHING FOR EPIC ADVENTURES, TALES OF SUSPENSE AND IMAGINATIVE WRITING THEN SEARCH NO MORE! YOUR HUNT IS AT AN END WITH THIS ANTHOLOGY OF MINI SAGAS.

We challenged secondary school students to craft a story in just 100 words. In this first installment of our SOS Sagas, their mission was to write on the theme of 'Hunted'. But they weren't restricted to just predator vs prey, oh no. They were encouraged to think beyond their first instincts and explore deeper into the theme.

The result is a variety of styles and genres and, as well as some classic cat and mouse games, inside these pages you'll find characters looking for meaning, people running from their darkest fears or maybe even death itself on the hunt.

Here at Young Writers it's our aim to inspire the next generation and instill in them a love for creative writing, and what better way than to see their work in print? The imagination and skill within these pages are proof that we might just be achieving that aim! Well done to each of these fantastic authors.

So if you're ready to find out if the hunter will become the hunted, read on!

CONTENTS

LIPA Sixth Form College Mount Street, Liverpool

Emerson Jennings (17)	58
Robert Paterson (14)	59
Erin Woods (13)	60
Mia Jones (13)	61
Adam Joseph Riley (15)	62
Niamh Andrew (16)	63

Manchester Islamic Grammar School For Girls, Chorlton

Maryam Khan (12)	64
Iman Mahmood (12)	65
Maria Jawad (11)	66
Zainab Mohiuddin (12)	67
Muskaan Shahid (13)	68
Areej Ali (12)	69
Maziyah Shaikh (12)	70
Hannah Laiyba Iqbal (12)	71
Hawwa Haq (11)	72
Anum Khan (11)	73
Hafsah Khan (13)	74
Manaal Siddiqui (13)	75
Fatimah-Noor Naveed (12)	76
Sama Sweed (12)	77
Hafsa Ahmed (11)	78

Teesside High School, Eaglescliffe

Henry Hunt	79
Ellis Leon Ettridge (13)	80
Grace Dye (13)	81
Amelia Mae Storey (11)	82
Matilda Ainsley (13)	83
Sophie Annis (13)	84
Thea Poole (13)	85
Lydia Wilson (13)	86
Alvaro Varela Escobedo (12)	87
Rachael Turner (14)	88
Lucy Mulcrone (12)	89
Barnaby Hawkings (11)	90

Charlotte Sowerby (13)	91
Luke Robinson (11)	92
Roman Khalili (12)	93
Davy Johnson (13)	94

Villiers High School, Southall

Sanika Kiritharan (13)	95
Agreem Pradhan (13)	96
Nadal Makoto Spencer-Jennings (12)	97
Sanaja Sivakunar (15)	98
Deepshika Kamalakasan (11)	99
Nusayba Bendjaglouli (11)	100
Killien Mohamed (13)	101
Rabia Ahmed (11)	102
Zayna Mozam (11)	103
Arshmeet Singh Turna (11)	104
Deshan Rai (12)	105
Jay Lakshmi Amichande (11)	106
Diya Patel (12)	107
Munazza Khalid (13)	108
Tarnbeer Singh (13)	109
Gurveer Singh Thind (11)	110
Jevin Dias (11)	111
Aaron Singam (13)	112
Inaya Ahmed (11)	113
Freddie-Jay Sinclair (12)	114
Freya Ahmed (12)	115
Lizann Barretto (13)	116
Whysnaie Mangaleswaran (11)	117
Rohit Narvekar (13)	118
Ambika Vaishnavi Gautam (11)	119
Ranjana Rani (14)	120
Sion Thomas	121
Asma Abdo (13)	122
Zain Naeem (12)	123
Mabel Barreto (15)	124
Amina Aden (11)	125
Vian Kenrich Fernandes (16)	126
Alisha Choudhry (13)	127
Alishba Aslam (12)	128
Jasmin Sandhu (12)	129
Nimit Aswin (11)	130

THE STORIES

Bloodbath

What started as a game has now become a bloodbath. A massacre. My heart cannot stop beating, I'm overwhelmed with thoughts and feelings. Am I going to die? Are my friends still alive? Her dark presence consumes the atmosphere and she lurks over her victims like a dragon protecting her eggs. There is an elephantine steel door trapping me inside this pitch-black room. There is only the tiniest bit of light filtering through the minuscule window. Her menacing footsteps creep towards the door, gradually growing louder and louder. In this final moment, I know I am going to die.

Cerys Nicholls (13)
Bromley Independent Grammar, West Wickham

To The Top

With a whistling swoop and loud bangs, bombs hit the base. Walls cave in on me. Pulling myself up, I'm unhurt but I can hear the guard dogs barking. I run! The elevator is broken. I have to climb up an old rusty ladder. It's pulling away from the wall. The gunshots get louder and the elevator starts moving. The lift's coming up towards me. I climb even quicker and the elevator hits the roof. *Bang!* Slamming shut the service door behind me on top of the shaft, I see moonlight. I run into the woods. I'm free!

Samuel Garratt (13)

Bromley Independent Grammar, West Wickham

Hunted

They're coming, it's got to be here. The key, it has to be here. My friends all gone, trained into troops for the monster army. They're going to make me into a brainwashed soldier. It must, I put it here, I must have. It's open, but how? It must have been pried open. It's dark in the corridors of the manor house. Also, there is a dark lantern lit by bugs. The exit is guarded by ghoulish monsters who are not good enough to fight. The last job is to get past the monster guarding the exit...

Eleanor Raynor (12)
Bromley Independent Grammar, West Wickham

Black Friday

We were close. The prize item in our grasp, yet in such a quiet Walmart, the doors opened and it began. Suddenly, a roar as if starving lions came out of their den. People were screaming, scraping for anything their hands could grab, including us and our new console. We raced through the sea of the dead as a flock of people came in attacking us and pecking away at our things. We calmly, quietly, assuringly ran, then out of nowhere, when we got to the till it hit me. *Oh God, it's Black Friday!*

Tarell Etsetowaghan (13)
Bromley Independent Grammar, West Wickham

The Police Chase

Friday night, I went out, got drunk, and decided to drive myself home in my Audi SUV, speeding at 100mph. The police started chasing me. I turned around and started shooting at the police with my AK-47 and the police started shooting back and hit my car. I smashed into an enormous tree and passed out. I took out my gun again and shot countless times at the police and I stole their Ford SUV. The car was powerful. When I pressed the gas pedal, it jolted forward. I drove fast towards the sunset. I was free.

Samuel Abraham (13)
Bromley Independent Grammar, West Wickham

A New Phone Maybe...?

I only had three hours, I had to make it to the sun. I had to get it, I had to find one. I encountered lots of people on my way there, I pushed them out of the way on the urge to find it. I could see the sun in the distance. I ran up the stairs as fast as I could, desperately trying to reach it. Finally, I could get it, that new phone. Finally, I could get the new iPhone 1,100,000 Pro. It was my time to shine, I looked towards the sales counter, they were gone...

Nailah Kascia Robertson (12)
Bromley Independent Grammar, West Wickham

The Hunt Is On

"Huh, huh?" Vlad palpitated as a mix of emotions ran through his head, reminding himself of the mortals who were after him.

Crack! A twig snapped. Without wasting any time, Vlad fled from that area at once.

"Hey, come back here," a voice came from behind.

Vladamir ran faster than lightning as the mortals were quickly tracking his footsteps. Suddenly, his thirst for blood grew and took control over him. Vlad ran towards the men after him. The humans were confused and stood with their weapons in hand.

Vlad then screamed out very loudly, "I am Dracula... Count Dracula!"

Arni Kumar (12)
Guru Gobind Singh Khalsa College, Chigwell

Puzzled

Where am I? Wind consumed the overhanging trees. I was encased in a metal container. It smelt of rust. I was strapped down to a wooden chair. I couldn't free myself from my restraints. Then I had an idea. Briskly getting up, I forcefully backed into the wall and broke the chair. I ran out, all I could see was an expanse of forest, desolate trees, virescent grass monotonous clouds. I couldn't remember anything... *who would want to hurt me?* I scrutinised my surroundings, I spotted a flashing light... It was following me everywhere I went. Was I being hunted?

Neel Payesh Sobhun (12)
Guru Gobind Singh Khalsa College, Chigwell

No Turning Back!

My heart beat as fast as light. Sirens wailed across the streets. I regretted stealing that purse but there was no turning back. I concealed myself behind the elongated trees. "Come out! We know you're there so step forward with your hands in the air or face the consequences!" the policemen bellowed.
I regretted my decisions. I came out of a bunch of trees and leapt on a bike in my way. I cycled to freedom.
"Hurry up boys! We got prey to catch. Go go go!" the head policeman roared in anger.
The terrifying and intimidating hunt commenced.

Aahaan Srivastav (11)
Guru Gobind Singh Khalsa College, Chigwell

The Dark Stalker

Breathlessly panting, Lola ran as fast as lightning through the dark woods. The howling wind blew the trees to their death. Cold raindrops dripped on her head. Something was coming closer and closer. The crunching in the leaves got louder and louder. She stopped. The cold blackness was upon her. The moon was glittering in front of her. Suddenly, a black figure jumped out of nowhere. She fell back in fright. On the top of the cliff, the black figure charged towards her. Gunshots shattered her, leaving her no choice to jump. Her eyes closed forever, leaving her spirit.

Fawaaz Khan (14)
Guru Gobind Singh Khalsa College, Chigwell

Hunter Vs Hunted

The emergency broadcast system was playing. It said, "All citizens out there, there has been an incident where all of you have to try and survive before you get hunted by the disease which has been controlling people's minds. May the hunt begin."

I had to run with my mum and my sister, we all found some shelter that wasn't very durable. The roof collapsed after a second. So we had to keep running, we saw so many people being eaten and some becoming suicidal, it was scary! After, my mum started slowing down and got run over. I screamed.

Marissa Kaur Dhillon (12)
Guru Gobind Singh Khalsa College, Chigwell

Death Chase

I still have nightmares about it. Sirens wailed through my deafened ears repeatedly. Bright white lights violently flashed through the gloomy and foggy evening. I could remember it being like a classic hide-and-seek game, but the seekers weren't usual seekers, all they had in their brains was to kill. My heart pounded with my head spinning, very lost. All I could do now was run for my life. Literally. I visualised two escape routes and I was ready to run, still hearing their footsteps. It was now or never, before it was the end of my life.

Aaron Grewal (14)
Guru Gobind Singh Khalsa College, Chigwell

The Last Call

I felt it, he shot him. Dead. He was an innocent boy. Why would someone do such a horrific thing? On 18th November, after school, a man shot an innocent fourteen-year-old, dead. Why?
After they did the investigation, the man and the boy's dad were having issues. The parents couldn't handle the stress of their only child dying. So they decided to shoot the man that killed their son. When they went to his house, he stabbed both of the parents. The police came and shot the man dead. The police found out an innocent boy was hunted.

Dara Singh Baryah (11)
Guru Gobind Singh Khalsa College, Chigwell

Twenty-Four Hours To Live

I had twenty-four hours. I had no idea where I was. It was just cold and damp and very dark. I started to remember. The TV news. It said something about an asteroid hitting Earth without possibly being prevented. I then remembered getting super drunk. Well, whatever, I had to get home in time. I just ran straight. Continuously running, non-stop. There were voices in my head saying that I wouldn't make it in time. I stopped. So out of breath, I puked. It was then I knew I wouldn't make it. I prayed when as asteroid zoomed over me...

Manat Kumar Saraow (13)
Guru Gobind Singh Khalsa College, Chigwell

The Person

I still have nightmares about it. My weekly smoke in the woods. I'd often hear weird noises, but animals lurked near. First, the footsteps crushed the leaves. I reached into my pocket and cautiously pulled out my phone, flashing the dim torch. A dark figure cast its shadow over my fear. Silence. Unfamiliar thumps pounded in my chest, drifting up my throat as I encased myself in spine-chilling nausea. The humanoid trudged towards me. My narrow lungs strained, shoving out a blood-curdling shriek. I had no one, I was out of time.

Jeevan Lally (12)
Guru Gobind Singh Khalsa College, Chigwell

YoungWriters
Est. 1991

The Look Out

We were close but not close enough. Nearly. We were getting closer each second. The mysterious crime was nearly over. But we still needed to get to the other side or else we would die, so would everyone else. So close. I was thinking to myself, *would everyone die or could I get him?* This was such a horrible crime. Why would anyone even think of nuclear bombing a whole country? I then got a message that said, 'Look on your right and if you don't, you'll die'. So then I did and it was him. Would I catch him?

Harnik Singh Baryah (11)
Guru Gobind Singh Khalsa College, Chigwell

The Chase

Icy fingers gripped my arm in the darkness. I felt deep breathing on the back of my neck that sent an eerie chill down my spine. I turned around. I saw the most grotesque, diabolical, bloodthirsty beast I had ever seen. Fear impaled me. It let go of me and I ran. I ran through the withered, frosty, sodden dead grass. I accidentally tripped on something. I turned my body to find it staring down at me. Blood drained from my face. My heart pounded out my chest. My body began crippling. I was being chased, I was wanted, dead.

Devin Patel (12)
Guru Gobind Singh Khalsa College, Chigwell

My Job

We were deep in the forest and were directly behind him. We only had our sense of sound to help with finding this man, it was too dark to see anything. As the helicopter flew above us, helping find the criminal, we began to realise that the forest leads right onto the motorway. We attempted to avoid the infinite amount of trees and logs, before hearing glass shatter from a few metres ahead. It was him. Two cars were hit in the process. We looked to check on the passengers, for me to see my family crushed in the seats...

Simar Pardesi (14)
Guru Gobind Singh Khalsa College, Chigwell

The Green Witch

I couldn't run anymore, I was out of breath. It was pitch-black. I could not see anything. I heard the nasty, green witch's cackle. The cackle got louder and louder. I ran faster and faster until I lost them. There was a ginormous wall in front of me, it was a dead-end! I was lost and scared. It was ice-cold. I didn't know what to do. I looked behind and saw something moving. It was the witches. There was no way out. They got closer and closer. I had to do something. The witches had found me!

Ria Battu (12)
Guru Gobind Singh Khalsa College, Chigwell

The Two Choices

I had twenty-four hours to make a choice, either to go inside the old, mysterious house or to go inside the enormous maze. I ran rapidly inside the enormous maze and the only thing I kept on hearing were the police sirens. I knew it was dangerous to stay so I ran rapidly and I started getting overworked. I tried to find a way out but I couldn't. It got dark so I took a nap somewhere.

When I woke up, I knew that I needed to get out. The police sirens got louder. I knew that I was hunted.

Gauthama Thewwahandi (13)
Guru Gobind Singh Khalsa College, Chigwell

The Nightmare!

I still have nightmares about it. I go to sleep and I see nothing, pitch-black. I see something in the corner and go up to it, I ask if it's okay but no reply. I kneel down and try to look at its face but see nothing. I get up and walk away but I hear some whispers coming from it. I turn around and I see it behind me, standing up all dirty and messy. I step back but I step on a twig and it moves its head and runs towards me. I scream and fall down.

Jaya Kaur (14)
Guru Gobind Singh Khalsa College, Chigwell

Waiting

I woke up, I had breakfast, everything was normal. Nothing.
I was on my way to the park with my friend Daisy.
"Let's go a different way," said Daisy.
"Okay," I said, not being concerned.
We kept walking.
We got to a corner, we would normally turn left but Daisy said. "Turn right."
So I did. We kept walking.
"We're here."
I looked up. The woods. Me, trying to be cool, went in.
"Let's play hide-and-seek, you hide, I'll seek."
"Okay."
"One, two, three."
Nothing. Ten minutes. Nothing. One hour. Nothing. I'm Hannah, I just keep waiting.

Leonie D'Aguiar (11)
Hornsey School For Girls, London

The Culprit, The Hunter

"This is your next culprit," the voice bellowed.
I stared at the photo, the name.
"Okay," I whispered. There was something about his eyes, bright green.
"You have to leave, now!" the voice yelled.
Shivers tickled my spine. I had twenty-four hours. Swiftly, I equipped everything I needed, tying my long hair into a tousled ponytail. Sprinting, I rushed out of the dark bunker, running, faster than ever before. I had always been a rapid runner. At last, I arrived at a dim alleyway, and there he was, his hair shone in the darkness. I aimed the gun. *Bang!* Dead...

Vera Soran (12)
Hornsey School For Girls, London

The Game

Adrenaline ran through my body like a shiver of fear as I gripped tightly to Dina's hand, dragging her with me through the forest of shadows. I clumsily tripped over creeping vines, throwing myself into barbed brambles. I tried, with difficulty, to ignore the sharp pains which followed my recklessness. Mist swirled around us like distended fingers. With an increasing distortion, it crept around us. The beasts with pelts of black shrouded themselves in the impassable mist preventing us from escaping their deadly grasp. We ran towards what could be our inevitable demise. In a way that might be better.

Roxanne Ruth Suplee (13)
Hornsey School For Girls, London

Pest

I was trapped. Locked inside a gigantic test tube. Waiting for my friend to release me. Suddenly, he dropped from the ceiling and freed me.

He whispered, "We have to leave now."

I clambered out of the window and ran. *Boom!* The facility people had shot my friend down. I didn't care anymore. All I cared about was surviving. I suddenly broke into a sprint. I ran like never before. I could hear the security guards running after me. I climbed over the facility fence and ran. Until a voice in front of me shouted, "Going somewhere, pest?"

Yuna Lam (10)
Hornsey School For Girls, London

The Twin Sisters

It wasn't meant to happen, it just did and it all began when I was still in Mother's stomach. You see, growing up, my life wasn't easy. So when I heard the news that I had a twin sister but she had died in the womb, my life turned upside down.

One afternoon as I was getting ready for school, I heard someone or something call my name faintly.

"Abby, Abby," she whispered.

"Wh-Who are you?"

"It's me, your sister, please help me. I'm stuck in the underground world and all you have to do is give me your soul!"

Nada Moulana (11)
Hornsey School For Girls, London

The Hunters

The sirens wailed, we only had a few minutes before they arrived. The tables began to shake like a stampede heading towards us. Everyone started to panic as they ran for the door but I knew better and hurried towards the window. Gunshots and screams could be heard from outside, they were getting closer. The door handle turned and I leapt into the air, hitting the fragile glass. Millions of glass shards scattered around me but I didn't move, I didn't open my eyes, I didn't even dare to breathe. For everyone knew, you couldn't be spotted by... the hunters.

Tamsin Manceau (11)
Hornsey School For Girls, London

The Hunted

The potent smell of ash was lingering in her nose; meaning, she was close. She ran, exhaling hot air. Her chest felt tight. She was not losing another one. He was not getting away. Not this time. The fires had already been set to lead her astray before, but she was now on the criminal's tail. Seconds away from grabbing what was rightfully hers, she reached her arm out, extending it as far as she possibly could. She made a grab, her fingers intertwining, the creature being stolen from its home. Suddenly, everything went dark. She had lost him again...

Hafiza Khan (13)
Hornsey School For Girls, London

To Hunt Or Not To Hunt

The rain dripped onto the windshield as it swiped left to right. My car parked in front of the emerald green leaves. My AK-47 lay on my seat. *Cazar o no cazar.* To hunt or not to hunt. With my childhood best friend, Vicente, Canada is where it all happened. He set me up for death.

Before Abuelo passed, he told me, "Don't do it."

He looked at me, holding my hand saying, "Make me proud, Mateo. I'll be up there watching you."

He's the only one who loved me. Ten years later, here I am, hunting for him.

Nana Adebi (14)
Hornsey School For Girls, London

Devastated

I still have nightmares. I'll never forget the look on his face. Car chase. Everyone knew what happened but not how I felt, it was the most horrible feeling, it was like my churning insides got stabbed 'til I couldn't breathe. I remember we were running. Running for our lives. We'd reached the end of Tennon Road and the car door flung off and scraped my brother in the leg. Blood everywhere. He fell. I couldn't stop running. Then I heard that sound, skidding wheels. That was the last I saw of my twin brother. My heart was devastated.

Lila Alvarez Prasad (11)

Hornsey School For Girls, London

The Hunted

The moon lit the night but instead of watching proudly, it cowered behind the rolling grey clouds like they were the only thing shielding it from the horror to come, and a horror there was. An army of men stood before me.
"Are you a hunter or the hunted?" someone demanded.
I didn't reply.
"He is the hunted!"
Then savage wolves were released. They ripped me apart and tossed me into the sea. As I plunged into oblivion I wondered, *how many others have suffered this?* As I faced the seafloor, my question was answered, dozens...

Thea Le Neveu (11)
Hornsey School For Girls, London

The Hunters

Sweat trickles down my face, clouding my eyes. I don't have much time. Lifeless fingers surface from the fog and grasp at my shaking legs, but a whispered voice in my head pulls me on into the mist. I hear the disembodied footsteps of my pursuers echoing in the void behind me. I don't have much time. The metallic taste of blood lingers on my tongue, the gash on my cheek flowing dangerously freely from my earlier encounter with my hunters. If I don't escape, outwit, outlast them then everyone I hold dear to me will fall away into oblivion.

Alexa Swinhoe (11)
Hornsey School For Girls, London

Heartbeat

It all started on Halloween night... Me and my friend were on our way to a haunted house. As we were queuing up, we saw people running out screaming in a cold sweat. Me and my friend laughed as we thought they we all exaggerating. After a few minutes, we went in. Unfortunately, we were separated as the house was one at a time. There I was, alone in a haunted house. There were a bunch of jump-scares but I wasn't amused. It was then when I saw it, a man with a bloody knife...
He grinned and laughed, "Heeheehee..."

Tori Lei Teape (11)
Hornsey School For Girls, London

Below The Stars

The cold of the starless night was pinching my skin raw. A siren wailed in the distance. Time to hide. Dragging the corpse along the cobbles of the pavement was my only chance to escape. Blood splattered in all directions like an overflowing pipe. Looking up at the stars, I realised my only hope. Heaving the manhole cover to my shoulders, thoughts blurred through my head like an old black and white film. *Surely underground was the safest place?* I flung the body into the sewer, now light from the loss of blood. I had a chance.

Vitoria Soko (11)
Hornsey School For Girls, London

Run

Run. This word wasn't too familiar in the past. But now it was all I knew. It was the norm. To be honest I wasn't a natural-born runner. But doesn't humankind always adapt for its survival? Change when change must be made. *Isn't it ridiculous how all promises are broken when every man acts for himself?* How ruthless a parent must be to abandon their child for their own viability. And so, I was here, running. Running from what I feared but not dared to acknowledge. I lived alone. I ran alone and I would surely die alone.

Khadidja Cheref (14)
Hornsey School For Girls, London

Hunted...

Breathe in, breathe out. It hadn't been long since I heard the crinkling of the leaves. I wasn't sure what was out there, but I knew what it wanted. There was a sudden thump on the wall opposite me. My half-eaten dinner still had hot steam coming from it. All I could think about was getting out of this wretched town and escaping its creepiness. I shuffled to my bed and grabbed the walkie-talkie. My muffled cries for help crackled through the icy night air. No answer. Suddenly, I heard the ominous click of the latch. The door opened slowly...

Tabitha Archer (11)
Hornsey School For Girls, London

Hunted

On a stormy morning, Aisha, and her brother Ryan, woke up and found themselves in a whole new dimension with no one around them. As they were there, they decided to explore where they were. They found a creepy, old playground with an archaic house but, little did they know, they were being watched! Since they had no shelter whatsoever they approached the house. As they set foot in, they were attacked by vampire bats and had to run back as the door shut. It was a sign to leave. Suddenly, they woke up sweating from the dream they had...

Ishrat Shitab (11)
Hornsey School For Girls, London

Her Hidden Side...

She always smiled, just as bright as a sunflower. She walked angelically and many people, including me, admired her. She came from Japan and taught everyone about it! Her name was Blank, and she was the 'Goddess'.

There had been a murder near her apartment, everyone was worried about her... So we cheered her up, we had a party in a restaurant and tons of people got drunk, not me, though I probably looked like it. She told us all she was going to drive us home. However... we arrived. I ran for my life. She was the murderer.

Ariana Lay Cibej (11)
Hornsey School For Girls, London

Alone

My skin blistered as the rough ground rubbed my feet raw. As I stumbled forward blindly, I eyed the drop in front of me. The deafening wails failed to cease as I plummeted down the ravine. Brambles clung to my patched clothes as I pushed myself out of the bracken cluster that had served as my crash landing site. Realisation loomed over me as the truth set in. Panic overtook my body as I scrambled onto my feet. Thorns dug into my heels as they pounded against the valley floor. I was finally alone and I wasn't sure I'd survive.

Georgia Lorian Haslam (15)
Hornsey School For Girls, London

The First Hung

Her lips would form words directed only to herself. She was with the soul of the weather. It wasn't discreet, but obvious. She was a witch. She was the first witch hung. I can remember every pinpoint detail of her trial. She floated; she didn't sink, she floated in the inch deep water. So we wrapped the rope around her neck and called it a successful hunt. A successful witch hunt. I whispered it to myself as her eyes gradually rolled back. The deadly gossip saw me. So now I stepped onto the stand. I was the second witch hung.

Fiona Hamilton (12)
Hornsey School For Girls, London

Time To Run

I was being hunted so I continued running as fast as a cheetah but really, I was exhausted as an ox (after a day's work in the fields). I stopped for a second, I hid behind a bush to catch my breath.

In the shadows, I saw a woman with a hunchback. As I was hunted by her spirit, my palms were sweaty. My heart was beating so fast. I couldn't even think. I just stared into the sky whilst I sat still as a statue until the strange woman looked at me and walked... and walked... and walked... "Arghhhhh!"

Grace Nsavata (12)

Hornsey School For Girls, London

A Hunt For A Hunt

Dreadful pain ran through my lungs with every breath of glacial air I took in. The rusty axe I wielded clumsily, now rested heavy in my frostbitten hand. My legs staggered tiredly through the abundant snow. He set off to the mountains as soon as I ambushed him. He couldn't be far; he couldn't be! After all, I almost managed to disconnect his left knee cap from his leg, and his right shoulder must be dislocated. I had to kill him. I had to put an end to his pitiful life. Or else they would put an end to mine.

Laura Neagu (15)
Hornsey School For Girls, London

The End

It was a Sunday night. Dark and misty. I was running for my life. Sweat dripped down my neck and my adrenaline pumping. I needed to get out. Turning from side to side frantically, I could see a human-like figure ahead of me. I knew there were more of these gruesome creatures lurking behind the crippled, now dead trees, waiting to hunt the prey. Everyone I knew and loved was gone. I had nothing to possibly live for anymore but I was doing this for them. I had to survive. Suddenly a morbid screech came from behind me...

Leah Morgan (13)
Hornsey School For Girls, London

Why Me?

I still have nightmares about it. My brother took the shot for me! I remember all of his blood on my hands. He was lying in my arms looking into my eyes as if he was trying to say something.

He tried catching his breath back and he said his last words to me, "Look out for yourself."

What did he mean by that? Today is one year since his death and I was going to visit his grave. I arrived at the cemetery and on his stone was paper.

It said 'Your brother was right. You better look out'.

Aushria Singh (13)
Hornsey School For Girls, London

Runaway Robot!

I was walking down the street. I felt it in the darkness, somebody was stalking me. I ran! Until I was no longer able to because I was out of breath. All of a sudden, I banged into a door, unexpectedly placed right there. A flash of light turned on. Standing in front of me was a human. She looked like she needed help since she had several tubes sucked onto her. I set loose all the tubes but she dashed out the room. I saw a sign saying 'Evil Robot!'.
"Find her in an hour!"
I was pressured!

Sasha Singh (11)
Hornsey School For Girls, London

Sirens

The sirens wailed. Adrenaline was rushing through my veins. I knew in my heart that I would get caught and take the punishment for what I had done. But in that moment, I didn't care. The sirens were edging closer yet but I longed to get further and further away. Flashbacks to the event were all I could think of. Blood. Pain. Fury. But I couldn't focus on that right now. I was a bandit. A runaway. My foot slammed on the accelerator as I tried to break free. I was nearer to escaping than ever before...

Kayla Budka-Fox (12)
Hornsey School For Girls, London

The Gunshot

All of a sudden, I heard a gunshot. I knew straight away that I was being hunted. At record speed, I dashed out of the back door and into the arms of the dark forest. Then again, a gunshot. But this time it was closer. Fear began to take over my body and I found myself running, running faster than I ever had before. A familiar scream echoed through the forest and that was when I realised that scream belonged to me. Carelessly, I tumbled through a river but I was too slow. A dark figure had grabbed me away.

Charlotte Schmitz (12)
Hornsey School For Girls, London

The Arrow

My hooves clashed against the carpet of leaves, twigs and greenery. He was gaining on me. I struggled to keep calm. Adrenaline surged through me, coursing through my veins. As I ran, branches whacked my face and my antlers got caught in a vine overhead. I looked back. He was right there; he was drawing his arrow. In the moment that our eyes met, mine pleaded with him. But no; the brute had no mercy. The arrow sliced through the air. I felt it puncture my chest and I slowly dropped down to the floor, dead.

Naomi Cormacain (11)
Hornsey School For Girls, London

Voices

The moon was full and the fog that slithered by me was thick and moist. The bite of the late October night chilled me to the bone, causing me to shudder. The jacket that covered me was all I had when my car died on the side of the road. Few cars had passed me since then, all ignoring my plea to pull over. They simply looked my way, eyes wide and unseeing. Were they afraid of me? Was someone or something else out there? Suddenly, I heard a wolf howl in the distance. Would I escape this danger safely?

Sara Darwish (11)
Hornsey School For Girls, London

The Run

I couldn't run for much longer. I was being chased by people I didn't know, ringing loud sirens that blanked out my head. My mind was in a state of horror. I couldn't see anything. Everything was black. I kept running until I got to a forest. It was so big and dark but it was the only way to keep safe and away from them. I crept around the big maze then suddenly, I felt something on my shoulder. I slowly turned around and found a monstrous beast in front of me. I was caught...

Rawa Moulriche (10)
Hornsey School For Girls, London

Run Away

I couldn't run for much longer but I knew I had to if I wanted to get away from them. I didn't know what they wanted from me. From the first moment I saw them, evil intentions reflected off their eyes which is why I kept my distance, but somehow they were still able to find me. No one was around and my phone had also run out of charge. I was terrified and didn't know if I would make it. I needed to stop to catch a breath. But as I was gasping for air, my arm was grabbed.

Naimah Begum (13)
Hornsey School For Girls, London

Fooled

I threw the backpack over the fence, expecting to then be pulled up. I heard it land on the lid of the dumpster and clumpy boots scrambling to claim it then running away. I gaped there, in silence, trying to leap over the garden fence. It wasn't my garden. The only way I could rent a flat here in England was to make a deal with some people on the dark web (to steal drugs from a dealer). I landed back down with a thud. The owner heard me fall. Then a figure approached me...

Tayba Ahmed (11)

Hornsey School For Girls, London

I Thought I Lost You

I still have nightmares about it when she went missing... One day, me and Emma were playing hide-and-seek. When we used to play, I couldn't find her for a long time but I used to find her in the end. But then I got locked up for robbery and that was the last time I saw her when she was 6. I still hear Emma playing our favourite game.

One time, Emma was playing hide-and-seek and she went missing so I broke out of prison to go find her...

"I thought I lost you!"

Kiera Walker Brown (13)
Hornsey School For Girls, London

Escape

I couldn't run for much longer. My feet were debilitated and my breathing was heavy. I stopped. The sound of her faint footsteps was getting closer. I had to catch my breath but the time was ticking. I had to hide. And fast. I took all my strength to get back up and I started running in fear. Up ahead, I saw a small, familiar hut. I went in and locked the door. No sound.

My mind wondered where she was, up until I heard the three words, "I found you."

Anita Ndrejaj (14)
Hornsey School For Girls, London

Bog Boy

As the glowing moon illuminated the night, mist shrouded the noxious swamp, skeleton-like trees cast shadows in the murky waters and the winds howled and whistled. But all went quiet. Then... I heard it. Footsteps echoed my own, I was being followed. I ran as fast as I could, fear enveloped me like a dark cloud. I was blinded by panic. Cold wind rushed past me. My heart raced. Blood drained from my face. My brain repeated one word. Hunted. Hunted. Hunted.

Clara Figueiredo (10)
Hornsey School For Girls, London

The Last Human Being

The vulgar disease spread rapidly. Pain shot through my head like a dagger. I clenched my fists and gritted my teeth in an attempt at bracing myself against the instinctive pain. I gasped for air full of desperation and anguish. I knew I was safe for now. Many questions began to circle my head. *Was I the only one left?* I turned around casually and saw an eerie figure in the distance slowly approaching me. But he was not alone...

Isra Mohamud (13)
Hornsey School For Girls, London

On The Loose

I was on the loose. I sprinted through the forest. Every so often I looked behind to see if they were following me. Nowhere. I continued running, a throbbing sensation grew up my legs. My hair whipped in the air in all directions like loose threads hanging on for dear life. I paused, gasping as my ragged breath caught up to me. At that moment, mammoth arms grabbed me, muffling my defensive shrieks. I was finished. My fate was sealed...

Arissa Ahmed (11)
Hornsey School For Girls, London

Hunted

Time unravels like a Gordian knot. Precipitation persists, penetrating plant life and ploughing a deepening trench amongst the marsh. A single beam strikes through the spruce, it hits a... sound! A faun? Something more? It's hard to tell, no time to tell. Careful but quickening strides thread through the overgrowth, swerving unsteady ground and placing myself firmly behind a drenched fern. Perspiration. I take a second. Thoughts collect together momentarily. I don't know who, God knows why, but it's there... somewhere. I mustn't falter for much longer, for I know he pursues. I'm tired. Time unravels like a Gordian knot.

Emerson Jennings (17)
LIPA Sixth Form College Mount Street, Liverpool

Hunted

As soon as the seeker screamed fifty, we ran for it. The mile squared schoolyard was packed with kids running for their lives. They frantically split apart, like rain on a window. When the seeker shrieked nine, everyone was already hidden while constantly chatting. However, that all changed when the seeker opened the ground floor door. We all took our shoes off to reduce noise. I was still hiding on the ground floor, in a cupboard, with a hole. He kept getting closer. *Ping!* A harmony of phones led the seeker away. I was safe.

Robert Paterson (14)
LIPA Sixth Form College Mount Street, Liverpool

Hunted

I couldn't run any longer. I had to find shelter, or those zombies would eat me. I ran home as fast as I could. Fear was pouring out my veins. I didn't know where they had come from or why they were after me. I was relieved to see my block of flats, but devastated the zombies were charging behind. My phone had died! I was worried in case my mum was not safe, having no contact with her. I arrived and dashed into the lift. Suddenly, like a black blanket, zombies headed towards me. Was I going to survive?

Erin Woods (13)
LIPA Sixth Form College Mount Street, Liverpool

Hunted

My legs were in agony. I felt my bones snap after every move I made. People were coming after me, I regretted this. I'd just killed a guard, now I was getting away. Dogs and deafening footsteps, I needed help.
I'd been in prison for five years after murdering my mother. A very vicious argument occurred, she abandoned me from when I was born. She hated me. She left me every night to get drunk and left me with a takeaway. As I got older, my patience disappeared and that's what she deserved.

Mia Jones (13)
LIPA Sixth Form College Mount Street, Liverpool

Hunted

I still have nightmares about it, it has been two years today which makes me think about it even more. Footsteps crunching in the leaves. Hearing him breathe. What did they want me for? Whatever it was, I didn't do it. The attacker gained on me, had I collapsed I'd be dead. The knife was inches away and I knew it would be in my shoulders any second. Taking one last gasp and... silence. I turned round, he was dead on the floor. He tripped over a branch with the knife in his heart.

Adam Joseph Riley (15)
LIPA Sixth Form College Mount Street, Liverpool

Hunted

I had twenty-four hours and I couldn't run for much longer, or further. I was anxious and scorching, trying to find this child who was only seven years old. I couldn't believe the child had been kidnapped by this dangerous man. He was notorious for what he had done in his life. I knew I had to do this, but as I peeked around the corner, they appeared. "Hope, run here, quick! Let's go, I'll take you home and get him to court quick as possible."

Niamh Andrew (16)
LIPA Sixth Form College Mount Street, Liverpool

Assassinated

Footsteps sounded, closer than ever before. Terror stabbed. So close... so far. Centuries I'd sought revenge on the Emperor. The only one left. It was down to me to end this... The moment had arrived, but I'd hesitated a second too long. They'd found me, I clutched my venom-imbued dagger. Ten archways, nine hold back death. Thoughts flashed as the ominous sound drew nearer, success shrunk away and peril engulfed my soul. Doubt seated through my mind, an infection. Motivation entombed up above. Further than anyone? Too far, maybe. As they reached the archway, I knew. I tensed. And ran.

Maryam Khan (12)
Manchester Islamic Grammar School For Girls, Chorlton

Insidious Creatures

My heart was racing, fingers trembling and sweat was pouring down my face.

I had been running for a short time but it felt like decades.

I watched innocent creatures being trampled, leaving pools of blood behind.

It was manic.

Ravenous creatures pounded their feet and gobbled us like we were miniature sandwiches. They were insidious, killing anyone in sight.

What was going to happen next? Death, only if you were slow enough.

Danger lurked around the corner. I was petrified with every step I took. My only thought was, *will I survive?*

I was overcome with darkness...

Iman Mahmood (12)
Manchester Islamic Grammar School For Girls, Chorlton

Nightmares

I still have nightmares about it. They were coming. Their blood-curdling lips swam in my head. Their eyes were toxic gemstones that engulfed souls. I watched all the innocent people drop. They dropped down, chalk-white in terror. What could I... do? Who was I to help? I turned from my windowsill, I thought about my parents, how they'd dropped... cold to the floor. I wanted to kill them, after what they did to my parents. I would avenge them. I scampered down the staircase, opened the door. I dropped. Cold with fear. Sweat drooling down my forehead. I had failed.

Maria Jawad (11)
Manchester Islamic Grammar School For Girls, Chorlton

Doomed

I ran as fast as I could, sirens wailing noisily behind me. The closest thing was that dark, abandoned house. So I ran straight through the mysterious doors. I stood traumatised in fear, helplessly staring at the blood-curdling red stains on the walls. As I stood there, shaking, I heard the door creaking shut behind me. I was trapped! I pulled and tugged at the door, crying, wishing for it to open. *Why me?* I thought as I heard some strange whispering behind me. A shadow appeared. The figure grabbed my neck and squeezed and squeezed hard. I was doomed...

Zainab Mohiuddin (12)
Manchester Islamic Grammar School For Girls, Chorlton

The Girl And The Clown

There was a diminutive town. Almost insidious. A pragmatic girl was the only one left... or was she? She stood there. Still as a statue, breathing heavily, in the middle of nowhere. All you could hear was thunder, the wind was howling and the leaves were running away from 'it'.

Abruptly, a massive voice said, "I only want to play... come out from wherever you are."

She ran! She felt as if she was about to die. As she turned around, she saw the glossy and glistening nose of the creepy clown. He grabbed out a razor-sharp knife...

Muskaan Shahid (13)
Manchester Islamic Grammar School For Girls, Chorlton

The Sirens Wailed

The sirens wailed. I watched as everyone ran, panicking, trying to protect their loved ones. If you heard the siren, you knew that you only had a few hours to live. Every night, the ambulance would come, trying to save innocent people's lives. Some with blades or knives stuck in their throats. As soon as the siren stopped, it would mean one person was dead! The murder would only happen at night.
I went outside at 7pm. People running away. I was confused, I didn't hear any sirens at all. I looked behind and a person was holding a knife...

Areej Ali (12)
Manchester Islamic Grammar School For Girls, Chorlton

I Had Twenty-Four Hours!

I had twenty-four hours, it was ticking at a very quick pace. With every step I took, it started ticking faster and faster. My fate was sealed. *Tick tick tick!* That's all I heard. I didn't know what to do, time was running out. Without realising what I was doing, I took one small step towards the darkness. I could feel my sweat rushing down the back of my spine. My hands were trembling; my heart was thumping. Suddenly, I heard a huge explosion. *Boom!* What could it be? Where was it coming from? I was confused, lost and frail.

Maziyah Shaikh (12)
Manchester Islamic Grammar School For Girls, Chorlton

The Death Cure

I had twenty-four hours to find an antidote... to treat the most deadliest infection. At the end of the day, I was a hero or a murderer. Time was valuable, I ran around the street, searching for the hidden antidote, carrying the sick man with me. He had violent fits, his veins turned blue and blood oozed out of his stained mouth. Frantically running around, a strange-looking man started chasing after me, thinking that I was harming my friend. There was a blue container with... the antidote! As soon as I reached for it, a hand grabbed me...

Hannah Laiyba Iqbal (12)
Manchester Islamic Grammar School For Girls, Chorlton

Not Close Enough

We were close... yet not close enough. We were surrounded. Gasping for air, I ran. They were getting closer and closer. Through each step I took, they became faster. Guns cocked and the sirens stilled. So close... so close... I almost collapsed. We were a finger's touch away from the wall when all of a sudden, we heard a gunshot. One by one, after another, it was time... I pushed my group into the gap and with all my strength, I pushed the boulder to fill in the hole. As leader, I was most wanted. Now, here I was... trapped.

Hawwa Haq (11)
Manchester Islamic Grammar School For Girls, Chorlton

Hunted

The sirens wailed. I panted. Time was running out, I would be caught and sent to jail. The adrenaline rushed in my veins. I heard a car open.

"We have you surrounded!" called an ominous voice.

Was it the police? I was trapped. Nowhere to go. A boy in a dark cloak stared at me with his amber eyes. He sighed. Maybe he was on the lam as well.

He whispered one word, "Bye, bye."

I looked at him awkwardly. He dived inside his pocket. A sharp knife. I was trapped. That was it. I was doomed now.

Anum Khan (11)
Manchester Islamic Grammar School For Girls, Chorlton

On The Run

I couldn't run for much longer. I had no time left: two minutes, thirty seconds? My feet tripping over every rock that crossed my way. My hands were masked with blisters. Blood poured through my cuts and the sharp branches kept it from healing. My scars from previous hunts have been exposed. This was it. This was the end. The guns shot my way, slowing me down. I stopped. I couldn't run much longer. It was a dead-end. They were moments away from hunting me. I had no choice. I closed my eyes and jumped off the cliff.

Hafsah Khan (13)
Manchester Islamic Grammar School For Girls, Chorlton

Fear

We were close... Oh, so close and yet, so far. I ran. My body begged me to stop, but the adrenaline coursing through my veins told me otherwise. But I ran and ran and ran until the sound of her agonising scream hit my ears. Her voice pierced through my heart like a thousand knives and suddenly, I couldn't move. My mind went blank.
The last thing she said was my name.
I didn't realise the blade-like teeth in my neck until my warm blood started running down my back, a pit of regret in my stomach.

Manaal Siddiqui (13)
Manchester Islamic Grammar School For Girls, Chorlton

The Maze

Where am I? Where are we? Last thing I remember was me, Peter and Eva in hospital. I was surrounded by tall, black walls. A black mist had appeared out of nowhere. It was rushing towards me. My first instinct was... run! Left or right? Was this a maze? No, it can't be. My dream. The dream I had last night. It was repeating itself, but in real life. This screeching noise came from behind me. A scream, I remembered from my dream. I knew I couldn't escape this. I had to fight it. I had to kill it.

Fatimah-Noor Naveed (12)

Manchester Islamic Grammar School For Girls, Chorlton

Dead End

It was too late. They found us. We were surrounded. We'd been running from the police for the past hour. I had to think fast. Suddenly, I jumped onto a big rock and jumped over the policemen. I ran for my life and went into a dark alley. I could see the policemen. A few minutes later, I could see a wall in the distance. There were no turns. It was a dead-end! I tried jumping but it was too high. The police approached me. I heard them yelling. He aimed a gun at me and pulled the trigger...

Sama Sweed (12)
Manchester Islamic Grammar School For Girls, Chorlton

I Couldn't Run For Much Longer

I couldn't run for much longer. I couldn't. But she was my best friend, we played hide-and-seek all the time. Just why? Why her? Questions raced through my mind. She lay dead on the floor, only fourteen. Tears rolled down my face. I couldn't stop crying. I yelled for help, screaming. My body was shivering. The wolf ran away. I could see, in the distance, a man, dressed in black. I thought he was holding a stick. He came forward. Little did I know, it wasn't a stick. It was a gun. I was next.

Hafsa Ahmed (11)
Manchester Islamic Grammar School For Girls, Chorlton

Going Dark

An SAS team have been tracking dangerous Russian gas. The team includes Captain, Price, Kyle, Garrick, whose mission is to safely return the gas. As Price and Kyle head to Urikstan, they come up against another terrorist group who are trying to get the gas. The gas was last located in a hospital where it is being held by terrorists.
After raiding the building, the two soldiers get into a gunfight with the rebels. *Bang!* A bullet strikes Price in the shoulder and is quickly rushed away and the mission is cancelled and everyone is evacuated away from the war.

Henry Hunt
Teesside High School, Eaglescliffe

The Alien's Escape

I sprinted through the woods, the bright glare of strobe lights slowly coming closer. My breath became more harsh, my speed starting to dwindle. My objective was in sight, the space grey metal of my ship slowly becoming clearer. I sprinted as fast as I could, the sounds of humans crunching leaves as they ran becoming more apparent. I had reached the yellow and black outline of the landing strip. The glare of the moon reflecting off the futuristic, shiny, glowing paint of the spaceship. I scrambled inside and calmly walked to the cockpit, sat down and pressed launch.

Ellis Leon Ettridge (13)
Teesside High School, Eaglescliffe

Days, Weeks, Hours

I had now been running for hours, days, weeks. My legs aching, head banging and every inhalation feeling like pins stabbing the inside of my throat. I could hear it behind me, crushing everything in its path and replacing it with darkness. Lightning struck. I continued to run, lost in my thoughts.

"It's not real, it's not real," I said unconvincingly to myself.

It was a predator. Its eyes were better than any hawk and teeth sharper than knives. It was coming towards me at full speed. I was a statue, frozen with fear. Suddenly, I awoke from my nightmare.

Grace Dye (13)
Teesside High School, Eaglescliffe

Chased

I was stumbling. I couldn't run much longer. I heard blood-curdling screams behind me. He wanted me, just me, no one else. I heard someone behind me. It was him. I had run miles. I couldn't keep it up much longer. My legs felt like daggers hitting me every time I moved. I stopped to catch my breath.

Then I heard someone whisper, "You can run but you can't hide."

I couldn't move, fear got the better of me. A cold sweat down my neck, he was getting closer. Then I felt someone breathing down my neck. I screamed...

Amelia Mae Storey (11)
Teesside High School, Eaglescliffe

The Original

They say you can run but you can't hide. They are right. I've been running for days but hiding is nearly impossible. Every crunch of a leaf, every crackle of a branch, every noise, I panic and I run. I try not to but my body sprints before my brain can even jog. That's why they always find me, I can't hide. I peer from behind the stump. I see them but it's not like before, there's not one or two, there's groups with masses of members. Each looking eagerly around, high off the excitement and satisfaction of my death.

Matilda Ainsley (13)
Teesside High School, Eaglescliffe

The Device

I'm running away from everything I know. I'm twenty-eight, an ex FBI worker. I got the training and the contacts and went rogue. There are forces trying to find me but I have bigger problems: five gangs out to get me! A friend invented a life-changing device, they all want it. He hasn't the sense to get away and keep it safe, so that's where I come in. His invention, a battery, the size put in remotes, could power a whole city the size of London. There are highly-trained assassins everywhere. The best thing is, I loved it.

Sophie Annis (13)
Teesside High School, Eaglescliffe

The End

Fifteen years on the run, life couldn't possibly get any harder. Sleeping in the shrubs, along with drinking out of the filthy streams. I didn't know where I was but all I knew was that I was destined for a life worth living. I was now being surrounded by a circle of police. My journey was over and perhaps my life. I only killed the man, why kill another? Guns to the head. Surrender or die. Why? Life in prison or death in hell? If I surrendered, it would probably be a life sentence. Dying would be the end, forever.

Thea Poole (13)
Teesside High School, Eaglescliffe

Crumbling On The Hunt

The sirens initiated, the chase was on. I ran as fast as I could down unpleasant alleys and up hills. I ran like the wind but I just wasn't fast enough. I checked behind me and the sirens were piercing. I felt like giving up but on the other hand, I knew I needed to proceed. My life was crumbling right before my eyes and I felt worthless. All these years I'd hidden I could've made a new life but no, I stayed the same. At that moment, I heard shouting and voices and I knew I couldn't give up...

Lydia Wilson (13)
Teesside High School, Eaglescliffe

Chased In The Forest

I couldn't run any more, the murderer was following me. It was dark, surrounded by trees. The murderer was like a very big, fat troll with a gun. He shot. He didn't aim too well and hit a tree. Another person was running away from the murderer. His name: John Churchill. He fell down and the murderer caught him. I heard him shout. I was getting to the town, I could see the skyscraper. I called the police. After a few minutes, I heard the sirens. One policeman with a gun shot the murderer. He lay on the floor.

Alvaro Varela Escobedo (12)
Teesside High School, Eaglescliffe

The Hunt

The sirens started, I could hear them getting closer. I ached all over. I felt like I was going to collapse but I knew I had to keep going. I wouldn't let them catch me. I could still see all the blood, all that pain in her eyes. But I couldn't concentrate on that now. I had to get away from this place. I scrambled through the bushes, my legs cut and bruised. I was beginning to lose hope, there was no one for miles. I was alone. I felt like I was walking forever and would never stop. *Bang!*

Rachael Turner (14)
Teesside High School, Eaglescliffe

Captured

I couldn't run for much longer, they were chasing me! I was trying to hide but I could hear them coming. I went running through the woods, fields, roads. I even got chased by a cow! Which was very scary. I did all that, just so they wouldn't catch me, but I thought I was far from the catchers now, so I didn't have to worry.

The next day, they were stood outside of my tent. They told me to get in their big, black Mercedes and took me back into their office. I had to get out of here!

Lucy Mulcrone (12)
Teesside High School, Eaglescliffe

Escaped And Ran

I had thirty minutes to reach the airport because I just escaped Area 51 and now I could hear sounds catching up to me. Apparently, there were aliens who lived there. I was on a road, walking in a line but then I turned around and there were five figures not moving, but staring at me. Suddenly, I made a run for it. A few seconds later, I tripped, the figures caught up to me. I thought it was the end but they were other people who escaped. They took me to the airport where the flight took me home.

Barnaby Hawkings (11)
Teesside High School, Eaglescliffe

Trapped

I can see the fence rising 200 metres above the city, spikes along the top and barbed wire covering every centimetre of metal. In the dark of the night sky, the moon highlights the fence perfectly. It is a death trap. How am I going to get out? All I know is that I have to get out of here, out of this city, this prison, this web of lies. I am a fly caught in a spider's web. At the bottom of the fence, is where I now stand. I have no other choice. I start praying and climbing...

Charlotte Sowerby (13)
Teesside High School, Eaglescliffe

Run For Your Life

I had to keep running away, I couldn't let them get me. They had guns, what did I have? I had nothing. I needed to find a weapon, food, water and shelter. I was a fugitive, I shouldn't have had a weapon. I could hear them, I could see their guns, they knew who to look for. I ran as fast and as far as I could, until I tripped. I almost tripped off a cliff, they were above me but seemed to have not noticed me. I was hanging there, but I could not hold on any longer...

Luke Robinson (11)
Teesside High School, Eaglescliffe

Hunter

I can't run for much longer. One guy is trying to hunt me. I have been running for hours but the person has a gun. I am trying to hide in the trees, behind their huge trunks and in their brown and green leaves. I think he has gone so I run as fast as I can. I finally find a village and she's there. I get into the car and she drives me to another city. A man hands me a new passport, with a new identity. I walk off into my new life. He can't catch me.

Roman Khalili (12)
Teesside High School, Eaglescliffe

Fugitive

I groped about in the mud, trying to find the device. In the distance, I heard the wail of sirens and the drone of choppers. I hadn't got much time! I ducked into the brush to avoid a chopper's searchlight. As it passed me, I saw a glint of light and made for it. As my fingers closed round the device, I heard the screech of tyres then a squelch of boots in the nearby mud. A searchlight fell on me. I was surrounded! I pressed the button to teleport...

Davy Johnson (13)
Teesside High School, Eaglescliffe

Hunter Or Hunted

I silently stalk the hooded figure, trying to focus on the task but my mind keeps wandering, imagining the rewards I'll get for exterminating humanity's greatest threat.
"When you start your life, it starts a journey."
I pull out a gun and smile, I edge closer.
"You shall run, it shall walk."
I fire the gun and smile triumphantly, it's gone.
"You shall rest, it shall not."
I call HQ, when I feel a cold hand on my shoulder.
"One day, you'll make a mistake."
I spin around and see it advancing quickly, smirking.
"Your life will then be over..."

Sanika Kiritharan (13)
Villiers High School, Southall

Criminal Mastermind

Pablo Escobar, criminal mastermind, escaped. Twenty-four hours began now. Seen last at the border.
"He went that way."
Twenty-four carats of gold weren't going to get away so easily at the border of Mexico.
"He went that way to his house," said the witness.
BM7 FD1. Escobar's home. I went in, gun ready. I swiftly passed what looked like a kitchen and crouched against a wall. Where had he hidden his gold? I crept up to his bedroom. Bingo! All the gold was there. Then...
"Stop!" shouted a man behind me.
100 men circled me. I had become the hunted.

Agreem Pradhan (13)
Villiers High School, Southall

Project S.W.A.R.M.

Secret Weapon Aerial Ripper Maniac is what S.W.A.R.M. stands for, a bad thing, made by bad people. Of course, our air-headed community thought this was a bloody good thing, because of some lie about it protecting us from the 'Code-Z8' operation. I knew this was fake news, and that Project S.W.A.R.M. would be uncontrollable and needed to be stopped! But what could I do, I was just some farm girl.
"Warning! The safety systems have been breached. Please go into full lockdown! This is not a drill!"
"See, I knew it!" I said to my friend.
Silence, then... *roar!*

Nadal Makoto Spencer-Jennings (12)
Villiers High School, Southall

Inescapable

A hundred metres away to finding myself digested inside a rickety stomach. My torso ripped, my trachea tightened, one breath seized in, the threatening barbarians were attracted to me like a magnet. My falling arms glued securely onto my stomach, my eyes were a dimming street light. The barbarians snarled. My shivering body darted around vigilantly. Ten of them huddled around me, examined me as if I was a roasted chicken. Showing one of them aggressively, my silky hands transformed into inky, veined hands. They crawled closer and closer, I had no other option but to run for my life...

Sanaja Sivakunar (15)
Villiers High School, Southall

Miracle!

Sirens! Running through the forest, I feared for my life! *Nothing can happen*, I thought. My life was at great risk. I didn't do anything wrong. All I could hear were sirens! Never-ending sirens. Before I could do anything, a policeman stood right in front of me.

I pleaded, stating, "I didn't do anything!"

Policemen never trust us since all criminals say that. My life was over. But I never gave up so I started running, running for my life without any doubt. I had no one with me right now. Then, I saw something, something I could not believe...

Deepshika Kamalakasan (11)
Villiers High School, Southall

The Sleepover

I'd just woken up from my sleep, remembering that I had school today. It was a school were girls wore puffy skirts and boys wore blue jumpsuits. I put my uniform on and headed to school, thinking about how fun the sleepover would be.

After school, I headed to my friend's house. We started talking about demons and how powerful they were when suddenly, the power went out. We then started hearing footsteps upstairs. One of the girls decided to check it out. Minutes later, we heard loud screams upstairs. Out of nowhere, we found blood dripping down the stairs...

Nusayba Bendjaglouli (11)
Villiers High School, Southall

Origins

It all started in WWII, the Germans and the French found a spot between Italy and Austria containing a mysterious element that was blast-proof but had side-effects, some were loss of memory and nausea. It didn't matter. They named it Element 115. They thought if they could build a robot, they would win the war.

D-Day arrived and Germany sent out the robot to protect the German Empire. With a crew of twenty-five, they were killed and the robot destroyed. But suddenly, the crew became the undead and attacked. Any man that died was turned. But hope was still alive.

Killien Mohamed (13)
Villiers High School, Southall

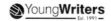

Haunted

I couldn't run for much longer, desperate, I screamed for help.

"Please someone, anyone help, help!"

I was exhausted, afraid, terrified, torn, running away in the jungle from predators or beasts who were hunting me. I had no choice but to remain emotionless and keep my pain inside me otherwise they could sense my fear of them. My heart was pumping furiously because of my fear inside me. My body starting to ache, my head started to beat really hard as it was painful and I was scared that something was going to happen. I knew I would be hunted.

Rabia Ahmed (11)
Villiers High School, Southall

Run Or Hide

Now they know. They know I'm gone. They know I know their secret, I have to leave now. My legs are falling asleep. Oh God. They're here. I'm trying not to breathe. They are looking at the other end of the room. My time to escape has come! No! The vase falls and shatters into millions of little fragments. They edge towards me. I find a gun. Finger on the trigger, I creep out of my hiding space.

"Stop!" I shout.

They stare at me.

"I'm armed and you're not," I say. "Back away now, and never ever return."

Zayna Mozam (11)
Villiers High School, Southall

The Hunted Night

My arms and legs felt as if someone was chopping them off. My heart was a beating drum. I was panting like a dog as I ran as fast as the wind. Then... the sirens went on. My palm sweating. My heart thumping. Hesitantly, I snuck into a narrow passageway.

"Shhhhh!" exclaimed prisoner number 145. "Do you want to get out of here or not?"

As I crept behind him, a torchlight shone everywhere. Anxiously tiptoeing past the guards, we... Nightmares still rush through my mind about that horrific, hunted and haunted, treacherous night. For now...

Arshmeet Singh Turna (11)
Villiers High School, Southall

Dark Times Upon Us!

Twenty-four hours... The Dark Forces were going to destroy the Earth. So, we prepared for battle; guns, bombs, planes fully loaded. I'd spend quality time with my family, just in case I never see them again. Walking like a turtle, I fell asleep again. Hours later, I woke up, being very energetic and there was a few minutes until they arrived. I could see the empire marching at us. Continuous lightning bolts struck around us and all the animals were going wild. We were ready to fire until a grenade flew at us. It was a force field. "Fire! Attack!"

Deshan Rai (12)
Villiers High School, Southall

Midnight Sleepover

Today, my life has changed totally. I still have nightmares about it.
I couldn't run for much longer. We were trapped. The sirens wailed. That night was the worst. I still remember the frightening noises surrounding me. One by one, my friends disappeared. I could still hear them screaming their heads off. My legs burned, my torso ached, every inhalation felt like needles stabbing my throat. I remember I woke up in the middle of nowhere. My friends were taken behind the old wooden oak tree. All I could see was blood, but nothing else. I had escaped the forest.

Jay Lakshmi Amichande (11)
Villiers High School, Southall

Chase 101

I had twenty-four hours to escape from the bank but could I make it? I felt nervous and thought I was going to get caught. One step further and the police would catch me. One step away and I would've been safe and... frozen. Suddenly, I heard my friend's voice, "Erica, run now!"
"Arghhhhh!" I screamed.

Out of nowhere, a cop grabbed our money and joined us on the run. We were petrified, thinking he would take us in but he didn't, it turned out that he was in trouble as he murdered someone in the police station.

Diya Patel (12)
Villiers High School, Southall

Found You!

"Hide-and-seek!" screeched my deadly nightmare.
I couldn't run for much longer, my legs burned, my torso ached, every inhalation felt like needles stabbing down my throat. The siren wailed, it wasn't safe. I only had a few seconds. It was now or never. I shot through the wind like a bullet, yet somehow it snatched me in the middle of the air, and dug its sharp claws within me, scratching my skin off. I lay motionless in my blood and stared at my despair reflection, as everything blacked out. Suddenly, I awoke to a cold, slimy drop.

Munazza Khalid (13)
Villiers High School, Southall

Final Strike

We have twenty-four hours to find the terrorist in the desert. Let's get our troops ready to attack on this base. It's 15th June, it's boiling in the desert. As we're approaching the base, an ambulance draws near us to check us. They try to kill us so we get into a gunfight. After a long gunfight, we clear the area but the terrorist receives the news and tries to escape. We are chasing him. After a long chase and firing, we abduct the terrorist and take him to America. I say, "Mission accomplished," and I am thrilled.

Tarnbeer Singh (13)
Villiers High School, Southall

Cops And Criminals

Twenty-four hours. That's all I have got. It's dangerous out there. But unfortunately, I have to go. As I walk out onto the dark, gloomy woods, he spots me and now, he calls his friends. They are behind me, I knew I should have got some weapons or been armed. Now the cop has called for back-up. So, I start running. That is a really bad idea. He shoots me straight in the leg.

"Arghhhhh!" I shout in pain.

Suddenly, I see a shadow, it is Jeffy, my friend, helping me to my feet.

"Will we escape?" I ask Jeffy.

Gurveer Singh Thind (11)
Villiers High School, Southall

The Zombie Invasion

Twenty-four hours to find out the infection about the zombies and about the bloodthirsty werewolf. The night was silent, we were nearly at the lab. Then we started coursing towards the lab's entrance. There we saw how they turned humans to zombies and werewolves. Then we tried to steal the chemical.

Suddenly, two zombies attacked us, we took the chemical and ran for our lives. We knew that they would hunt us to get the chemical back. Then we walked and fell from a hill towards a road. A car came zooming towards us and told us to get in.

Jevin Dias (11)
Villiers High School, Southall

The Haunting

The story started with a group of friends going into this haunted mansion, they told themselves to stay together but they could tell someone was missing. Then suddenly, they could hear a scream. They all tried to run out but believe it or not, the door was locked.

"How are we gonna get out of here?" a boy exclaimed.

Before he was dragged away screaming, they tried to pull him. But it was too late.

There were two left, a boy and a girl. They looked around, they could hear snarls from behind them. They turned around...

Aaron Singam (13)
Villiers High School, Southall

Escape

I was packing as fast as I could, they were trying to break down the door now, and we were trapped. My friend was still sleeping on the couch, so I jabbed him as hard as I could and then he woke with a start.

"What the heck?" he said.

Then he heard the banging and shouting, his eyes went wide with fear.

"It's them isn't it?"

I nodded. He jumped off the couch and thrust his shoes on. I snapped the suitcase shut. Then we ran down our escape passage into the cold night. We were safe, for now.

Inaya Ahmed (11)
Villiers High School, Southall

The Thing

It's been a good day. After being promoted to chief of medicine, I have just returned from a celebration party. The previous chief had passed away two weeks earlier and I feel guilty for taking his place so early on.

I get shivers crawling down my spine, it doesn't feel like a normal shiver. It feels evil and angry, it feels like I'm wanted dead. I feel eyes watching me from the corner of the room. Immediately, I fly back to the sofa, I can't move. A skinny rake-like... thing, crawls towards me and climbs on me...

Freddie-Jay Sinclair (12)
Villiers High School, Southall

The Werewolf Had Lost His Rare Blood

I couldn't run for much longer as the werewolf was chasing me all night. I had twenty-four hours left to defeat this wild creature before me. My legs ached because I had been running all day and I hadn't had a break. My friend was with me, but it wasn't safe now they knew. Now, everything was going to be all wrong. Eventually, me and my friend were trying to kill the hideous werewolf that was always close to my fresh blood. We found the werewolf, and each time we stabbed him, it became weaker and weaker 'til his death.

Freya Ahmed (12)
Villiers High School, Southall

Dark Aura

I automatically found myself running but I was somewhere else... wait! I looked at my body, it wasn't mine, I even had a tattoo. It had numbers: 3114. Did it say 'Ella'? Or something... When I turned back, there was nothing, just dark black woods. Why was this person running? It was weird in this new body. I got used to it. Just had to find out more about this person. Suddenly, I heard footsteps, I wasn't alone. The moment that person sharpened something, I was paralysed, every nerve and cell through me stopped. He started speaking...

Lizann Barretto (13)
Villiers High School, Southall

Remembering WWII

The sun came down, the moon was up. I was tucked in bed as my mum kissed me goodnight. It hit 12pm. Once I woke up as the sirens wailed, my mum banged and pushed the door until I opened it.

"Wake up! Go to the basement!"

Once I took a look at her face, I knew something was wrong! We ran down to the basement as our family huddled. My heart was rumbling, I could hardly breathe. I felt the pain down my throat like something was stabbing me. *Boom! Crash* went the bombs. Quietly, we stayed, breathing silently.

Whysnaie Mangaleswaran (11)
Villiers High School, Southall

Catching The Culprit

We were close.

"Find him."

If we didn't find him, he would hunt one more animal. He had to be somewhere over here. We had to leave now, it was too dark, it wasn't safe to stay here in the dark.

"Let's come tomorrow."

We came in the morning but he was not there, we waited for him 'til night but he never came and again, tomorrow morning, I went over there and I found him. He was searching for animals to hunt and I saw him. I ran to him and I caught him and took him to prison.

Rohit Narvekar (13)

Villiers High School, Southall

The Nightmare

Sirens wailed... my heart was pounding and I was shivering. I stood up and looked around me, it was dark. Tears rolled down my eyes. I had no idea where I was. Blood was dripping down from above. I looked around a bit more to see cut-open bodies. Suddenly, something caught my eyes, it was something bright... I leaned forward a little more. *A man?* I thought, *no...* I was worried. *Oh my God! Someone's here!* So I ran the opposite direction, thinking I would lose him. Out of nowhere, he turned around...

Ambika Vaishnavi Gautam (11)
Villiers High School, Southall

The Doll

I was reading a book. It was about a witch doll. She was a really good doll. But scientists did too much research which affected her and she became scary, haunted. She started killing people. She kept using other people's bodies and started hurting everyone. And on her face, there was blood and something pure white which made her look more scary and bad. At midnight, she made a loud noise and if any animal or bird saw her, they started crying loudly. When any traveller passed her, she would wait patiently and then kill them.

Ranjana Rani (14)
Villiers High School, Southall

Snakehead

I'd run for miles, my chest, legs and ribs felt like they were about to explode. The criminal organisation, Snakehead, were on to me. They want my brain to create robots of their own. Where my right hand was is just a stump.

Just as I thought I was making progress, I heard a chopper above. Its light was shining above me, blinding me completely. I waited for the bullets to sink through me but no, I looked back and they were releasing a ladder down to the ground. I soon realised what they were doing and ran towards them.

Sion Thomas
Villiers High School, Southall

Lost And Found

It was unexpected for cars to come by, it was dark and very quiet, until a strange man came out of his cheap car, pointing at me. I was confused and scared as he came closer.

"What do you want?" I screamed as he offered no explanation.

He stared into my eyes whilst he reached for his pockets. I tried to escape but there was no exit. He stabbed me as I screamed.

"Stop!"

I felt the knife going through my stomach. There was no help. I'd woken up in a hospital, I had been lost and found!

Asma Abdo (13)
Villiers High School, Southall

The Haunted House

I still had nightmares about the haunted house. It was too hard to forget about what I saw in front of my eyes.
The next day, me and my friends decided to go back there because we wanted to stop people from getting scared by entering the house. Looking around, we saw that there were cameras, but the previous time we came here, there weren't any - however, there was a pool of blood. Upon exploring more, we saw a creature and we thought that it was just an illusion, but through a mirror, we saw the ghost behind us.

Zain Naeem (12)
Villiers High School, Southall

The Sound Of Death

It's not safe now they know my hiding place. As I step outside, my life drops like the temperature. I'm in fear of getting killed because I'm abnormal and like to kill people when the frustration is out of limits.

Suddenly, I hear the sirens wail. I sprint like a cheetah. My heart starts running as if it is in a marathon with me. The fear of losing my life makes me realise how precious life is. I can feel my hands trembling as I sprint, I can taste my death. I cannot free my burning aura. It is trapped.

Mabel Barreto (15)
Villiers High School, Southall

124

Spirit Moans

In the dark and weary area, moans a spirit in its haunted doze. Nobody has identified this dreadful monster and what he is doing to us. He steals kids on the night of Halloween. When his portal opens, he takes them into his unknown world and tortures them with his bare hands. I have seen it with my own eyes. Who knows what he might do next? He might capture adults and think they are stronger so he can take them into the cruel world of his. What happens if these kids never come back? They might disappear there forever.

Amina Aden (11)
Villiers High School, Southall

Toxic

The sirens wailed, they knew we were the last men standing in the crumpled city. The toxic gases from the collapsed buildings would strangle us to death. We sprinted across the city so that we could get rid of these harmful gases. Unluckily, one of our men got caught up by the choking gases. Both of us didn't know how we were going to escape these gases. Further down the road was a river. We gasped for our lives. We both leapt into the river. I came out of the water like a dolphin and saw my friend disappear...

Vian Kenrich Fernandes (16)
Villiers High School, Southall

Anonymous

Who was this person? My phone was exploding with messages from someone called 'A'. It had now been going on for a while. Was I the only one getting these messages? Yes. I asked everyone I could if they had been receiving anonymous messages.

Finally, I decided to chase A down, but how was I supposed to? Every step I took, A was ten steps ahead. Everything I thought of, A had already thought of it. Who could it be? What did I do to deserve this? Finally, I had found a way to A. The hunt had finally begun.

Alisha Choudhry (13)
Villiers High School, Southall

Animal Hide-And-Seek

I couldn't run for much longer, my delicate legs started to ache immensely. My heart was pounding rapidly whilst I was running. When I stopped to have water, a berry popped out from nowhere. I was really curious about who threw the berry at me. I looked behind the bush myself, and it was a cute, fluffy, white cat that had just had baby kittens. She was trying to get out of that place but she couldn't, so I picked her up and she gave me a nice, small cuddle and she was very tired so I took her home.

Alishba Aslam (12)
Villiers High School, Southall

Capture

It's not safe now they know... I never wanted to be like this, I never meant to cause harm. I keep on running through the forest, hoping they won't find me. I feel lonely, why am I like this? I'm a vampire. They don't understand, I'm going to be used for an experiment. I run with my vampire abilities, hoping to get away. As I am running, I manage to escape from them. I come upon someone. Someone who is just like me, finally, I'm no longer alone. Together, we run and go somewhere no one can ever find us...

Jasmin Sandhu (12)
Villiers High School, Southall

Criminal

I could hardly breathe. My legs hurt. I kept running. I could hear sirens. They were looking for me. I couldn't get caught. I had stitches. I tripped. I was hiding. I started to run. I could see the cops looking for me. I kept on running. Five hours later, I reached the city. I had a little bit of money. I changed my clothes because the cops had seen my clothes. They, fortunately, didn't see my face. I hoped they didn't see my face. I came out the shop. I saw cops. I had escaped from the cops.

Nimit Aswin (11)
Villiers High School, Southall

The World Depended On Me

I need it. I need it now. I sprint through the woods. There is no turning back now. There are puzzling obstacles to get through. My heart is beating as fast as the wind. The world is depending on me. I watch the world crumble behind me. The wind howls as my precious locks cover my face. The rain pours down and thunder bursts my ears. Hell is waiting for me. I am not going to give up easily. Then I see the light. The purple sparkling gem. My hands trembling, I hold it up. I've saved the entire world...

Shaymaa Abdalla (11)
Villiers High School, Southall

Thought

We were running when one of our friends got lifted up. There were sixteen of us and now there were twelve. One by one, we were hunted. It went from sixteen to fifteen to fourteen to four. Then I came face to face with it. There it was, the dark figure, using its thoughts to find us and take us back home. I tried resisting but remembered my mum and thought about her and how she didn't come home that night. Then the dark figure took off its hood and there she was, my sweet, loving, kind-hearted mother.

Adil Butt (14)
Villiers High School, Southall

The Survival Game

The sirens wailed and games began. I ran to the tiny hut and hid there. I heard the chasers run past the hut with their giant axes, ready to kill me so they could win the cash prize. I waited and waited. Then suddenly, I could hear someone approaching the hut, dragging their axe across the floor. I quickly leapt out the back window. He saw me and started chasing me. I ran for my life as my heart beat frantically. I was getting tired so I started to climb a tree. As he swung his axe, the sirens wailed.

Milan Binu (12)

Villiers High School, Southall

Hunted

My legs ached. Every inhalation felt like needles stabbing down my throat. I knew it was going to find me. I knew it was my end. Panting, I kept moving. I knew it wouldn't stop until it found me, took me to a world of its own. I ploughed through the ditch and collapsed on the other side.
I woke up behind this narrow tree. I turned my head to see it screeching. I was sweaty, nervous, my heart pounding! I had to escape, I just had to! I knew I had barely enough time. There was no turning back.

Riya Jately (12)
Villiers High School, Southall

The Unknown

I heard something smashing and roaring simultaneously, repeating himself. I didn't know what it was, so I quickly took a peek at it. It wasn't what I expected at all. It had a funny-looking hand. It had pink and blue spots. When he opened his mouth as wide as if he was about to eat the whole planet, I could see the black and yellow in his teeth and all the blood in his mouth. It was the craziest night I had. Nobody knew what he was or had in mind. It was best to call it 'The Unknown'.

Nathan Francis (12)
Villiers High School, Southall

The Unknown Night

It all started when I was returning from a shop at 12.30pm. It was all dark and someone pulled my bag. Inside the bag, there was £100.

I cried, "Stop, leave it, you thief!"

I ran as fast as I could but in the meantime, shockingly, someone was running after me. I realised it was a trick to send me away from the populated streets. I was confused about what I should do. Where should I go? The man was catching up with me, he looked like someone who hated me from childhood...

Haresa Habibur
Villiers High School, Southall

Most Wanted

I can't run any further. I have travelled a few miles from my prison and there's no time to give up. I have suffered enough and now I must escape. I am the world's most wanted man. But then, the sirens start to wail. I know they've found out I have escaped. Helicopters surround the circulating area. I wish I had just stayed in the cell. My family is far, far away and I just want to see them. But my time has come. I am running out of breath and saying my last words. I'm hunted.

Johan Virgil Mariyathas (13)
Villiers High School, Southall

Back Rooms

I don't know what happened. It felt like I'd been sleeping for years. When I woke up in a very weird place, I noticed the walls were yellow and it was dark. But there was very little light. Suddenly, my eyes opened in horror when I found out I was in the back rooms. The only place I never wished to visit. I saw a very scary figure there. So I ran in every single direction but I never found the way out, I just went in circles. A long time ago, aliens invaded it. I never escaped this place.

Kassuf Ridda Rana (14)
Villiers High School, Southall

Last Day

I don't want to live any longer. These nightmares have chased us to this abandoned zone. This zone is safe enough for us to stay well for the time being. Later on, out of nowhere, I see a red stain on my sleeves. I am panic-stricken. Even worse, I realise I am... bitten! the feeling of utter shock has collapsed me to the ground. My friends are all staring at me, and I know it from their face that they cannot risk keeping me alive. My friends have left me, I don't want to be one of them.

Michael Molla Degu (15)
Villiers High School, Southall

Stopping The Terrorist!

I had awoken, I was on a plane to Brazil. My partner and I were going to the main city, which is Brasilia. We were on a hunt to stop a right-wing terrorist from committing terrorism by bombing Brasilia. As we were informed by the police that he was last seen at 3.30pm, now it was 4.30pm, we were given an address to where he would be because we were gonna raid him.

After landing, we were at his house and we broke in. He was on his bed. We arrested him, but no signs of the explosive bombs.

Tanraj Saund (14)
Villiers High School, Southall

Zombies Attacked Us

One day in Harrow, at 12am on New Year night, I was coming back home from a New Year party. Me and my parents were ready to go home. While we were going to the bus stop, we heard weird noises. The noises sounded like zombies. We reached the bus stop, the bus came, we entered the bus and guess what... there was a zombie driver who was driving the bus. There were zombies on the bus, the door closed. We got scared, bodies shivering. They came to eat us. I shouted loudly. I woke up from my dream.

Anshawl Cain Desousa (14)
Villiers High School, Southall

Sister Hunt

I wasn't far nor was I close. I glared at the tall trees rustling in the wind. It was late at night by the time I had approached the forbidden forest. I had to find my lost sister before the sun rose. Otherwise, she would disappear. The moon shone bright just like it did in my nightmares. I was running out of time. There, in the distance, stood tall and anxious, it was my sister. The sun burst up. I had run out of time. My sister was dead, I sprinted out of my bed. It was all a dream...

Gabrielle Masih (11)
Villiers High School, Southall

Hunted

I couldn't run for much longer. I was exhausted. I was bleeding heavily from my hand and face. I was beaten up by the merciless people. I tried to look for a place to hide and keep me safe.

Forty minutes passed, and I thought I lost them. I was very tired and I needed to sit and take rest. I then sat down next to a gigantic tree. I was feeling very thirsty, so I went off to look for water. As I was looking for water, I heard footsteps behind me. It was them. I tried running...

Talha Adnan (15)
Villiers High School, Southall

Hide-And-Seek

Cold... dark... I was scared. I was being hunted by my own family. They all were playing a game of never-ending hide-and-seek. I was scared that I would die. My family was different, their eyes were bloodshot red. Their skin was pale as snow. They each wielded a heavy chainsaw. This was not normal hide-and-seek, it was a kill or be killed situation. Not like I knew how to kill anyway. I'd just been caught by my family and now I'd been caught, I joined them and you should too.

Arjun Singh
Villiers High School, Southall

The Wolves

I couldn't run for much longer. There was three of them. My heart was pumping hard. I had to leave, now. They were faster than cheetahs. Their greedy eyes were staring at me. Their sharp teeth waiting for me. It was the wolves. I couldn't stop for a second. I was so tired, but finally, I could see the daylight. It was an inch away from me. I stopped running. But they all jumped on me together. I felt only one of my legs, half my body was out of the forest and half was in.

Parman Manan (11)
Villiers High School, Southall

Zombie Apocalypse

I couldn't run for much longer. My legs aching, my throat dry. I was being chased by the zombies. We were so close to the safe house but then, one zombie leapt forward and held onto my leg. I was trying to shake him off but he wouldn't let go. He was trying to bite my leg but he had no teeth. All the adrenaline ran through my blood. I kicked him and he went flying into the others. Out of breath, I sprinted for my life. When I reached the safe house, I let out a big phew!

Hassan Shahid (12)
Villiers High School, Southall

The Killer's Plan

I couldn't run for much longer, my throat was dry and my head was on the verge of blowing up. I was terrified and what made me more scared was that I heard about fifty footsteps behind me, but I stayed my ground and started running. As I was getting closer to my house, I heard a ton of sirens wailing behind me then I realised I was getting chased by the killer who made everybody flee the facilities. The next time I was going to a party would be in a long, long time.

Ayub Jama
Villiers High School, Southall

Infected

I was on the run, the terrifying moaning of the infected was getting closer. I had to get to some place safe, then suddenly, I came across an abandoned shop that had everything in it: food, water, you name it. It was also a good place to stay. It was ten hours in and the sun was rising. I had to get on the move as swiftly as I could. I ran out the doors and headed to the closest village I could find, until I saw something shimmering on the floor. It was an old toy...

Noah Philbert (11)
Villiers High School, Southall

Someone Is Watching

I am miles away from them but they just won't have me. I need to run, I cannot stop but how far will I be able to go? I will have to stop sometime soon, it just is impossible to lose sight of them. They are everywhere. I am in a dark forest and I am even more scared right now. What if they make me one of them or kill me? They are here, I can hear them, their heavy footsteps are the only thing I can hear in the silence of the thick forest. They are watching.

Mishca Fernandes (11)
Villiers High School, Southall

The Countdown Has Begun

It has been three weeks, unknown, unfound. I have been escaping death. The monster within me has devoured my humanity. They have left me in the wilderness to die. The countdown of my death has begun. I was forged into a weapon but was too good for my own. They started to fear me and look at me with disgust.

"Monster!" they screamed.

The pain I endured was immeasurable. Heaven or hell, where would I go? Someone please just take my soul.

Kartik Nungwal (14)
Villiers High School, Southall

YOUNG WRITERS INFORMATION

We hope you have enjoyed reading this book – and that you will continue to in the coming years.

If you're a young writer who enjoys reading and creative writing, or the parent of an enthusiastic poet or story writer, do visit our website **www.youngwriters.co.uk**. Here you will find free competitions, workshops and games, as well as recommended reads, a poetry glossary and our blog. There's lots to keep budding writers motivated to write!

If you would like to order further copies of this book, or any of our other titles, then please give us a call or order via your online account.

Young Writers
Remus House
Coltsfoot Drive
Peterborough
PE2 9BF
(01733) 890066
info@youngwriters.co.uk